THE MYSTERY OF THE QUEEN'S JEWELS

created by

GERTRUDE CHANDLER WARNER

Illustrated by Charles Tang

ALBERT WHITMAN & Company

Activities by Nancy E. Krulik

Activity illustrations by Alfred Giuliani

ISBN 0-8075-5451-0

5 7 9 10 8 6 4

Printed in the U.S.A.

Contents

CHAPTER 1

An Exciting Phone Call

"I'll get it!" twelve-year-old Jessie Alden called, running for the telephone. She and her brother, six-year-old Benny, had been playing checkers in the living room of their grandfather's large house. Jessie reached the phone on the hall table just as it rang for the third time. "Hello?" she said, picking it up. "Yes, this is the home of James Alden. I'm his granddaughter." She paused, listening to what the person on the other end was saying. "Really? How exciting!" Jessie said after a moment.

Benny had followed his sister into the hall. He wondered who was on the telephone, and what he or she had said that was so exciting. He liked solving mysteries, even small ones like this.

"I didn't even know he was going away," Jessie said into the phone.

"Who's going away?" Benny said to himself.

"To London!" Jessie was saying. "I'll tell him as soon as he gets home. Thank you. Good-bye." She hung up the phone.

"Who was that? What's so exciting? Who's going away?" Benny asked.

"Slow down," Jessie said, smiling at her little brother. "That was Grandfather's travel agent. She said that his airplane tickets to London are ready."

"Airplane tickets!" Benny cried with excitement. "But where's London?"

"It's across the ocean, in a country called England," Jessie said.

"Did I hear you say Grandfather was going away?" asked their ten-year-old sister, Violet, who had just come downstairs.

"Yes, to London!" Benny said. "It's across the ocean, in another country!"

"Let's go look in the atlas, Benny, and I can show you exactly where it is," Jessie suggested.

They all went into the den, which was lined with bookcases. Their fourteen-year-old brother, Henry, was sitting in a large comfortable chair, reading a book. Their dog, Watch, lay curled up at his feet.

The children had lived with their grandfather ever since their parents had died. At first they'd been afraid of him and had run away to hide in an old boxcar in the woods. But once they met Mr. Alden they'd realized what a warm, loving man he was and had come to live with him. And he had even moved the boxcar to the backyard so they could play in it.

Jessie told Henry about Grandfather's trip. Then she pulled out the large leather-bound atlas from the bottom shelf of one of the bookcases. She turned the pages slowly until she found a map that showed the United States and England. "See, here's where we live." She pointed to the United States. "And here's England," she said, pointing to a small country on the other side of the page. "London is the capital city, just like Washington, D.C., is the capital of our country."

"What's all that blue in the middle of the page?" Benny asked, pointing.

"That's the Atlantic Ocean," said Henry.

"England looks pretty far away," said Benny.

"It is," Jessie said. "Grandfather's plane ride there will probably take at least six hours."

"Look," Henry said, pulling another book from the shelf. "Here's a guide to London."

The children gathered around Henry as he slowly turned the pages. The book told all about London, the sights to see and things to do. It had lots of glossy colored pictures. Henry turned to a page with a picture of a palace.

"What's that?" Benny asked.

"That's Buckingham Palace, where the queen lives," Henry said.

"Wow! A real palace, with a queen and everything!" said Benny.

The next picture showed a line of men marching, wearing bright red coats, and tall furry black hats on their heads. "Those are the queen's guards," Jessie said.

"Their hats sure are funny," said Benny.

"That's Big Ben," said Violet, pointing to another picture.

"Who?" Benny asked.

Violet giggled. "It's not a *who*," she said. "It's a beautiful old clock tower."

"And there's a double-decker bus," said Henry. "It must be fun to ride on the top of one of those."

"I bet Grandfather is going to have a good time in London," said Benny. "I sure wish we could go with him."

That night, when James Alden came home for dinner, his grandchildren were waiting for him in the front hallway.

"Your travel agent called today," Jessie said. "She told me —"

"We didn't know you were going away," Benny interrupted. "To London!"

"Yes, I have some business to take care of

there," said Grandfather. "I just found out myself." He took off his coat and hung it in the closet.

"I wish we could go with you," said Benny.

"You do?" Grandfather said. Nobody noticed the slight smile on his face.

"We found some pictures of London in a guidebook," Jessie explained. "It looks like a wonderful place."

"It's one of my favorite cities," said Grandfather, his smile spreading. "I think you'll like it."

"You think *we'll* like it?" asked Violet.

"Yes," Grandfather said, breaking into a big smile. "You're coming with me!"

"We are?" asked Benny.

"I guess the travel agent didn't tell you," Grandfather explained. "Those airplane tickets are for all of us."

"Hooray!" the children chorused.

A week later, their suitcases packed, the Aldens were boarding a large airplane, bound for London. It was almost nine o'clock at night. Grandfather had explained that they would sleep on the airplane and the next morning they'd be in England.

"We're in row three," called Jessie, leading the way. "We can put our backpacks up here, Benny." After putting her own backpack in the overhead bin, she reached for Benny's. He had packed all sorts of games and toys in his little red backpack.

"But I wanted to do some of the puzzles I brought," he said.

"Grandfather said we have to put everything away before takeoff," said Jessie.

She settled into her seat and helped Benny buckle his seat belt. Henry and Violet were sitting right across the aisle, and Grandfather was in front of them, reading his newspaper.

Just then, a man came rushing down the aisle. He was wearing a wrinkled suit and a raincoat. His arms were filled with newspapers, and over his shoulder was a red backpack much like Benny's. The man's face was flushed, as if he'd been running, and his hair was a mess. He stopped when he got to the third row, and dropped everything onto the floor. After searching in all his pockets, he finally pulled out a crumpled ticket. He looked at it, then turned to Henry and spoke softly with a British accent. "Excuse me. I believe you're in my seat." He held out his ticket for Henry to see.

Henry looked at the man's ticket. "I think you're in this row," he said politely, pointing to the seat in front of Jessie.

"I am? Yes, you're right. I'm so sorry," the man said. He looked down at his pile of things on the floor. "Oh, dear, what a mess."

"Can I help you?" Henry asked. "How about if I put your backpack up here?" He placed the backpack in the overhead bin.

"Thanks so much." The man put out his hand to Henry. "I'm Charles Finchley."

"I'm Henry Alden, and this is my grandfather, James Alden, and my sisters and brother, Violet, Jessie, and Benny," Henry said.

"It's our first trip to London," Benny said.

"It is?" Charles said. "London's my home. I'm sure you'll like it very much."

A friendly voice began speaking over the loudspeaker. "This is the pilot. Please take your seats. We're ready to taxi out to the runway."

Soon all the passengers were settled in their seats, and the airplane taxied out to the runway and took off. After a while the flight attendants came down the aisles pushing large carts filled with drinks and snacks. While the children drank their juice and ate their small packets of peanuts, they chatted with Charles and some of the other passengers about London. Charles suggested some sights near their inn that they might like.

The flight attendants came down the aisles and gave a set of earphones to each passenger.

"What are these for?" Benny asked.

"You plug them into the side of your seat," Jessie explained. "You can listen to music, or you can use them to hear the movie that's going to be shown." She motioned to the screen at the front.

The children all plugged in their earphones and enjoyed the funny movie. When it was over, they felt very tired. Grandfather had urged them to get some sleep, but they'd been having too much fun. Finally, one by one, the children curled up and went to sleep. They'd been so busy, they'd forgotten all about the puzzles in Benny's backpack, which was still up in the overhead bin.

The children were awakened a short while later by sunlight streaming through the small airplane windows. The flight attendants were passing out trays of breakfast: scrambled eggs, toast with jam, slices of melon, and orange juice.

"Are we there yet?" Benny asked hopefully, rubbing his eyes and yawning.

"Soon," Grandfather told the children. "Eat your breakfast and we'll be there in no time."

Just as Grandfather had promised, once the flight attendants had cleared away the trays, a voice on the loudspeaker told them to fasten their seat belts. They would be landing soon! The children peered out the windows excitedly at the countryside below.

At last the plane was on the ground. "We hope you've enjoyed your trip," the pilot said over the loudspeaker. "Welcome to London."

CHAPTER 2

Two Very Different Guests

After the Aldens got off the plane, they had to pick up their luggage and wait in a long line to show their passports. At last they were ready to go to their inn. Grandfather had arranged for a cab to pick them up, and the large boxy black car was waiting outside. The driver loaded their suitcases into the back while the Aldens got inside.

"Hey, what's going on?" Benny said all of a sudden.

"What's wrong, Benny?" Jessie asked, concerned.

"There's something wrong with the car!" Benny said.

"There is?" asked Henry.

"Yes, the steering wheel is on the wrong side!" Benny cried.

Grandfather chuckled. "That's how they drive here in England. And wait until you see — the cars drive on the left side of the road instead of the right!"

In a short time they arrived at the Cheshire Inn. It was a small brick building on a quiet tree-lined street. In front was a small rose garden surrounded by a brick wall.

A plump gray-haired woman came hurrying out to greet them. "Mr. Alden!" she called out in a distinctive accent. "How nice to see you!" She took one of Grandfather's hands in her own and shook it vigorously.

"Mrs. Brown, it's so good to see you, also. These are my grandchildren, Henry, Jessie, Violet, and Benny," Grandfather said. "Mrs. Brown takes good care of me whenever I visit London."

"It's been a long time since your last visit," Mrs. Brown said. "Come on in and I'll show you around." Mrs. Brown reminded the children of Mrs. McGregor, Grandfather's housekeeper back home.

She led the Aldens inside to a cozy wood-paneled hallway. "Here's where we serve breakfast each morning," she said, motioning toward the dining room.

Next she showed them the living room. "This room is for all our guests to enjoy. We have a chess set and a backgammon board, and plenty of books. Make yourself at home anytime." The children saw that someone was already doing just that. A tall red-haired woman sat on the couch reading a book. She glanced up at the Aldens, but instead of saying hello, she turned her back and burrowed even more deeply into her book.

"There are two other guests staying here," Mrs. Brown explained. "That's Donna Russo," Mrs. Brown said. "These are the Aldens, Donna."

"Hello," Donna murmured, not looking up from her book.

"They're American, too," Mrs. Brown went on.

"Mmm-hmmm . . ." Donna said, still not looking up.

"Where in the States are you from?" Grandfather asked.

"California," Donna said, continuing to read.

Then Benny piped up, "What are you reading? It must be good!" He soon realized he'd said the wrong thing.

Donna looked up and gave him a piercing stare. "It's none of your business," she said angrily, closing her book with a snap. Tucking the book under her arm, she walked past the Aldens and up the stairs in a huff.

The Aldens looked at one another, surprised at her strong reaction.

Benny looked at the ground. "I was just trying to be friendly."

"Don't mind her," Mrs. Brown said, putting an arm around Benny's shoulders. "That's just her way. Come with me and I'll show you your rooms."

The Aldens followed Mrs. Brown up a flight of stairs. At the top of the stairs were two rooms opposite each other. One was Benny and Henry's, and the other was Grandfather's. Around the corner was the room Jessie and Violet would be sharing. Across from their room was a closed door.

"Another guest is staying in that room," Mrs. Brown explained.

"Not Donna, I hope," said Jessie. "I don't want to run into her too often if she's going to be so unfriendly."

Mrs. Brown smiled. "No, her room is upstairs. Andrew Smythe is across from you, and he's very nice."

"And there are only two other guests?" Jessie asked.

"Yes, that's all," said Mrs. Brown.

"That's why I like this inn," said Mr. Alden. "It's small and cozy."

Each room was decorated with pretty flowered wallpaper and delicate lace curtains. The beds had carved wooden headboards and were covered with soft fluffy quilts.

"I'm sure we'll be very comfortable," Jessie told Mrs. Brown.

"Let me know if you need anything," Mrs. Brown said with a warm smile, and she went back downstairs.

"I'm going to have a hot bath," Grandfather said. "Then we can go get some lunch." He went into his room.

The children were just heading into their own rooms when a young man in a long raincoat came bounding around the corner and almost bumped into Violet.

"Dreadfully sorry!" he cried, backing up and taking off his dark glasses. "Are you all right?"

"Yes, I'm fine," Violet said.

"I didn't see you," the man said. He was very attractive and had a deep, rich voice.

"Maybe that's because you were wearing your sunglasses inside," Benny said.

The man smiled, and the Aldens saw that he had perfect white teeth to go with his sparkling brown eyes. "Right you are, young man," he said. He noticed that the Aldens were still carrying their suitcases.

"Have you just arrived? Let me help you." He took the suitcase Jessie was holding and carried it back to her door.

"Thank you," said Jessie. She introduced herself and her brothers and sister. "We're from —"

"Don't tell me — the northeastern United States," the man said.

"Yes! How did you know?" Henry asked, amazed.

"I'm very good with accents," the man said. "I'm Andrew Smythe." He looked at his watch. "Oh, no, got to run. I've an important appointment in the West End. I'll be staying here for the rest of the week — let's have a chat when I get back. Cheerio!" He gave the children another smile and then hurried down the stairs.

"Wasn't it amazing that he knew where we were from without our telling him?" said Violet.

"Yes," agreed Henry.

"I wonder what the 'West End' is," said Violet.

"Isn't it strange?" Jessie said. "There are

only two other guests here, and they're completely different. One is very rude, and the other is as friendly as can be!"

The boys had just gotten settled into their room when Grandfather knocked on the door and poked his head in. He had taken a hot bath and changed his clothes. "Ready for lunch?" he asked.

"Yes!" cried Benny. "I'm in the mood for a burger and fries!"

"I thought we'd get something a bit more British," Grandfather said. "Come on, I'll get the girls and we'll go to my favorite pub."

"What's a pub?" Benny asked.

"That's short for public house," said Grandfather. "It's a place where you can get food and drinks. Pubs are very popular in England."

The Aldens walked down the street to the Prince of Wales Tavern. It was dark and cozy, and a fire blazed in the fireplace. The Aldens sat down at a corner table and Grandfather ordered shepherd's pie and Cornish pasties for all of them.

"Yum, I love pie and pastries," Benny said. "But shouldn't we have lunch before we get dessert?"

Grandfather smiled at Benny. "Shepherd's pie isn't really pie," he explained. "It's like beef stew, with mashed potatoes on top."

"Sounds delicious," said Henry.

"And I ordered Cornish 'pasties,' not 'pastries.' " Grandfather went on. "They're meat, potatoes, and vegetables baked in a pastry shell."

"Mmm!" said Jessie.

"I'm not too hungry," Violet said.

"I'll order you a ploughman's lunch," Grandfather said. "I think you'll like it."

As they waited for the food, the children told their grandfather about Andrew. "He knew where we were from — even which part of the United States — just from hearing us talk," Jessie said. "How do you think he figured that out?"

"I'm not sure," said Mr. Alden. "Some people know a lot about accents."

"I thought it was kind of strange," said Henry.

"Oh, Henry, he was so nice," said Jessie.

Violet's lunch arrived first: a chunk of sharp cheddar cheese, a piece of crusty bread, and some pickles. There was also a small bowl of fruit chutney. "This is great, Grandfather," she said, trying a bite of the bread.

Soon the waitress brought the hot food. The pasties had a light, flaky crust, and the shepherd's pie was steaming hot. The Aldens were hungry after their long trip, and they ate eagerly.

After lunch, Grandfather suggested they visit the British Museum. "The rest of this week I'll be busy with business meetings, so you kids will be on your own to see the sights. But the British Museum has always been my favorite."

"Sounds good to me," said Jessie.

"We can take the bus there," Mr. Alden said, leading the children to the corner. After a few minutes a large red bus pulled up and stopped.

"Look," Benny said, pointing. "People are sitting up on top. Can we do that?"

"Sure we can," said Grandfather. "This is a double-decker bus, and that's the best place to sit. We'll have a great view as we're riding." The Aldens climbed on and walked up a tiny staircase to the top. From there they could see all around. The children could tell that London was a very old city. Most of the buildings looked as if they'd been built a long time ago. The streets were narrow and winding, and there were lots of small cars and boxy black cabs.

"This is our stop," Grandfather said after a little while.

The children followed Mr. Alden off the bus and into a giant building with columns and a wide staircase up the front. The museum was one of the largest they had ever been in. Huge halls were filled with ancient artwork and sculptures. Glass cases held old books and documents written hundreds of years ago.

Violet was especially interested in a display of silverware and jewelry from old England. There were beautiful necklaces, earrings, and rings. Some of them had even belonged to queens and princesses.

Everyone's favorite was the hall full of Egyptian mummies. The Aldens spent a long time looking at the giant painted coffins and the mummified bodies of the pharaohs.

"I can't believe these are thousands of years old!" said Henry.

"Look over here!" called Jessie. "There's a mummy of a cat!" The others raced over to see.

"Wow!" Benny cried. "They have really neat things here in London!"

"They sure do," Grandfather said. "And this is only the start. Just imagine what you'll discover in the coming week!"

CHAPTER 3

A Friend Stops By

When they got back to the Cheshire Inn that evening after they'd eaten dinner, Mrs. Brown was in the lobby.

"Someone came by to see you," she told them. "I was out, but my son was here keeping an eye on things. He left this note." She held up a piece of paper.

"Who was it?" Mr. Alden asked.

"I don't know," Mrs. Brown said. "His note just says, 'Tell the Aldens a friend stopped by.' "

"Who do you think it was, Grandfather?" Violet asked.

"I don't know," he replied. "The only people I know in London are my business associates. I don't really have any friends here in town."

"Could it have been someone from Greenfield?" Henry wondered. "Maybe someone else is vacationing here, found out where we're staying, and came by to say hello."

"Was the friend a man or a woman?" Jessie asked Mrs. Brown.

"What did the person look like?" Benny added.

"I don't know," Mrs. Brown answered. "As I said, my son was here while I did some shopping. I found this note here on the front desk. He's already gone home, but next time I talk to him I'll ask."

Benny's eyes sparkled. "Isn't that strange," he said excitedly as the Aldens went upstairs to their rooms.

"I'm sure there's a simple explanation," Grandfather said.

"I think it's a mystery!" said Benny.

Grandfather chuckled and gave Benny a hug. "Good night, my little mystery solver. And don't forget, breakfast is served at eight o'clock."

"We know *Benny* won't forget," said Henry with a smile. Benny had the biggest appetite of anyone they knew.

The Aldens said good night and headed for their rooms.

Henry and Benny had just put on their pajamas when they heard a door shut. Benny peeked out and saw an old man walking down the hall. He was hunched over and carried a cane.

"Hey, Henry," Benny whispered. "Look!"

"What?" Henry asked, turning down the covers on his bed.

"Never mind. He's gone around the corner," said Benny.

"Who has?" asked Henry.

"There was an old man in the hallway," Benny explained. "I wonder who it could have been. I thought Andrew and Donna were the only other guests here."

"The man was probably visiting one of them," Henry said.

"Maybe . . . but I wonder. . . ." said Benny.

"Stop looking for mysteries and go to bed," Henry said. And with that, he turned off the light.

The next morning when the Aldens entered the dining room, the other two guests were already there.

"Good morning!" Andrew called out.

Donna smiled stiffly, then looked at her watch. "Excuse me, I have to be going now," she said as she got up from the table.

"Where are you off to today?" Andrew asked her.

She looked at Andrew for a moment before answering. "Nowhere in particular," she said coldly and walked out.

"It's funny she's leaving so quickly to go nowhere in particular," Andrew commented.

As the Aldens were sitting down, Mrs. Brown came in carrying a tray laden with food. She put a large bowl of scrambled eggs and a plate of steaming hot sausages on the table. "There are some fresh scones, still warm from the oven," she said, motioning toward a napkin-covered basket. Then she turned to Andrew. "Here's your tea." She placed a small teapot in front of him.

"Thank you," Andrew said, pouring himself a cup.

Mrs. Brown went back into the kitchen, leaving the guests to enjoy their breakfast.

"What are scones?" Violet asked.

"They're like biscuits," Mr. Alden explained, passing the basket to her.

Violet pulled out a scone and saw that it was studded with sweet, chewy currants. "Mmm, these look delicious," she said.

"Try a bit of gooseberry jam with them," suggested Andrew. "Mrs. Brown makes it herself."

Mr. Alden found a *London Times* newspaper on the table and began to read. Andrew asked the children what they were planning to do that day.

"Our grandfather has a business meeting

near Buckingham Palace, so he's going to drop us off there," Henry said.

"You'll get to see the changing of the guard," said Andrew. "It's a jolly good show."

"What are you going to do today?" Benny asked him.

"I'll be in the West End," he said.

"That's where you were headed yesterday," Jessie recalled. "What is it?"

"That's the part of London where the theaters are," Andrew explained. "I'm there every day, all day."

Suddenly Jessie remembered the dark glasses he'd been wearing the day before, as if he hadn't wanted anyone to recognize him. "Are you a famous actor?" she asked.

A strange look passed over Andrew's face, as if he was trying to decide how to answer. "Yes, I am," he said at last. "Of course, being from America, you may not have heard of me. I haven't made it to Hollywood — *yet.*" He smiled broadly. "But I'm quite well-known here in England, on the London stage."

"What show are you in?" Henry asked.

"Well, I've been in lots of things. . . ." Andrew said. "*Phantom of the Opera, Cats.* All the greats."

"What are you in now?" asked Violet.

"What am I performing at the moment?" Andrew said.

"Yes," said Violet.

"Um, well, it's, um . . ." Andrew paused for a moment and sipped his tea. "It's called . . . *The Mystery Man.* Yes, that's it."

"Are you the star?" asked Benny.

"Yes, of course," Andrew said.

"We're planning to go to the theater Thursday night," Jessie said. "Maybe we'll go see your play."

Suddenly Andrew looked uncomfortable. He put down his teacup and stood up abruptly. "Oh, yes, well . . . it's quite popular, so you may have trouble getting tickets." He laughed nervously. "I'll see you later." He picked up his raincoat and walked out quickly.

Just then Mrs. Brown came in. "Andrew, do you need more —" She stopped and looked around. "Has Andrew left already?" she asked the Aldens.

"Yes, just a moment ago," Henry said.

"That's odd." She picked up his full teacup. "He never leaves without finishing his tea. Ah, well." She cleared away Andrew's dishes and went back into the kitchen.

"I wonder why Andrew left so suddenly," said Jessie. "He looked as if something was bothering him."

"It almost seemed as if he didn't want to answer any more of our questions," Henry said.

"I thought I heard him say he was an actor," Grandfather said. "He was probably just in a hurry to get to the theater for a rehearsal." Grandfather looked at his watch. "Speaking of which, we'd better hurry if I'm going to make it to my meeting in time."

The Aldens finished eating and went back up to their rooms to get ready to go. But the whole time, Jessie couldn't help wondering what had been bothering Andrew.

CHAPTER 4

Follow That Cab!

Back upstairs, Grandfather gave the children some British money. "You can't use American money here," he explained, handing them some colorful paper bills and some large heavy coins.

"These don't look at all like dollars," said Benny. "There's a picture of a lady on it."

"These are called British pounds," Henry told his little brother. "That's a picture of the queen."

"We'd better bring some things with us

today, like a map and our guidebook," said Jessie.

"Don't forget the camera," said Violet.

"And an umbrella, in case it rains," Grandfather suggested. "It rains a lot in London."

"We can put that stuff in my backpack," Benny said, running to get his little red backpack from next to his bed.

A little while later, the Aldens were waiting in front of the inn. Mrs. Brown had arranged for a car to pick them up.

"There's a cab," said Benny, pointing a little way down the street.

"I don't think that's for us," Grandfather said. "If it was, the driver would pull up to the door."

"Anyway, it looks as if there's already someone in the back," Violet pointed out.

"I don't see anyone," said Jessie.

Violet looked again. "That's funny. I'm sure I saw someone in there a second ago."

"It's strange the way that cab is just sitting there with the motor running," Henry said.

Just then another big black cab pulled up, right in front of the inn. "This must be ours," Grandfather said. The children got into the backseat, and Grandfather sat up front, next to the driver.

As they pulled away from the curb, Violet took a look out the rear window. "Now that other cab is moving," she said.

Jessie looked back, too. "And there *is* someone in the backseat. But it's funny — the person has his hat pulled all the way down over his face, as if he doesn't want to be seen."

"How do you know it's a *he*?" asked Henry.

"Good point," Jessie said.

"A mysterious stranger!" said Benny.

"You kids and your mysteries," Grandfather said, chuckling.

A few minutes later, Violet turned around and looked out the rear window again. "That cab is still in back of us," she said. The others turned to look.

"I'm sure it's just a coincidence," said Grandfather.

But when they checked a few minutes later, after their cab had made several turns, the other one was still behind them. "I think we're being followed," said Jessie.

"Do you think that person got in the cab and said, 'Follow that cab!' like in the movies?" Benny asked.

Everyone laughed. Before they could figure out why someone might be following them, they had pulled up in front of a tall, imposing gate.

"Here we are," said Grandfather. "Buckingham Palace." The children got out, but Grandfather stayed inside. The cab was taking him to an office building a little bit farther up the road. Grandfather rolled down his window. "Do you have your map?"

"Yes," said Henry.

"And you have the money I gave you?" asked Grandfather.

"Yes," said Violet.

"And you have the phone number where I'll be?" asked Grandfather.

"Yes," said Jessie. "We'll be fine. We'll take a cab back to the inn when we're through here."

"All right. Then I'll see you back at the inn at dinnertime," Mr. Alden said, and the cab pulled away from the curb.

"Hey, what happened to that cab that was behind us?" asked Violet, looking around. It was nowhere in sight.

"I guess it's gone now," said Jessie. "Come on. Let's go see the palace."

The children looked at the beautiful building on the other side of the large iron gate. "Wow," said Benny, looking at the rows of windows. "It's huge! Does the queen really live there?"

"I think so," said Jessie. "Let's see what our guidebook says." She unzipped Benny's red backpack and reached inside. She pulled out the book and flipped a few pages. "Here's the section about the palace." She read quickly and then looked up. "It says the queen also has some other houses. But see that flag?" Jessie pointed to the middle of the building. "That flag is flown whenever the queen is here."

In front of the palace were several soldiers, standing stiffly at attention. They were wearing brilliant scarlet coats with a line of gold buttons down the center. They had on dark blue pants, white gloves, and tall furry black hats. They carried rifles on their shoulders.

"Are those soldiers guarding the palace?" Benny asked.

"Yes," said Jessie.

"How do they stand so still?" Benny wanted to know.

"That's their job. They're not allowed to move or talk or even smile while they're on duty," Henry explained.

"I wouldn't like that job," Benny said.

"Can we go inside the palace?" Violet asked.

"We can see the staterooms," Jessie said. "But we can't see where the queen actually lives."

"Let's go!" said Henry.

The Aldens waited in line to buy tickets

and tour the palace staterooms. While they were waiting, Violet looked at the other people in line. Most were noisy groups of tourists with cameras. They were speaking many different languages. She could tell from their clothes and hairstyles that they came from all over the world. Everyone seemed to be happy and excited.

Then she noticed someone who didn't fit in. It was a person in a raincoat, standing alone and looking at the ground. The person had a hat pulled low over his or her face.

Violet wondered if that could be the same person she'd seen in the cab behind them earlier that morning. That person had been wearing a hat pulled low on his face, too. But before she could point him out to her sister and brothers, they had reached the front of the line and were being ushered inside the palace.

Violet soon forgot about the stranger as she looked around at the magnificent palace. The rooms were elegantly decorated with antique vases, carved furniture, and beautiful paintings of former kings and queens.

After leaving the palace they entered the Royal Mews, where the horse-drawn carriages were kept. The children had never seen carriages like these before. They were fabulously decorated with jewels and gold.

"Isn't it wonderful?" Violet said. "Royal carriages, just like in a fairy tale!"

Jessie was more interested in the horses. "Look at that big chestnut horse, and the white one with the long mane! They're so beautiful!"

"Let's go back to the front of the palace now," suggested Henry as they left the Mews. "They're going to be changing the guard soon."

"What does 'changing the guard' mean?" asked Benny.

"Remember the royal guards we saw in front?" Henry reminded Benny. "The same soldiers don't stay there all the time. When a new group of soldiers comes to take their place, they call it the 'changing of the guard.' "

As the children walked, Violet happened to look back over her shoulder. That was when she realized that the mysterious stranger was still behind them. But just then, Henry called out, "Hurry, it's starting!"

Violet ran to catch up with the others. What she saw when she got to the palace amazed her. There were no longer just a few guards standing stiffly at attention. Now long lines of guards were marching across the courtyard in front of the palace. They marched across the courtyard, lifting their knees high, in step to rhythmic drumbeats. It was very exciting to watch.

"That was great!" Jessie said when the guards were done marching.

"I'm going to be one of the queen's guards when I grow up," said Benny. He marched back and forth along the iron fence, lifting his knees high just as the guards had done. He pretended to carry a rifle on his shoulder. The others watched as Benny tried to keep his face serious like the soldiers. But it was too hard. Soon he burst

out laughing, and so did Jessie, Violet, and Henry.

"All this marching is making me hungry," said Benny. "Can we get lunch now?"

"Sure," said Henry. "Grandfather suggested we walk up this way to find a place to eat."

As Henry led the way, Violet remembered the mysterious stranger who'd been following them. She decided to peek over her shoulder one more time. She felt sure that he or she would be gone. He was probably just another tourist who wanted to see the palace and the changing of the guard. He probably hadn't been following them at all.

But when Violet looked back, there was no mistaking it. The person in the long raincoat was still walking behind them!

CHAPTER 5

A Secret Plan

"Look, a pizzeria!" Benny called out. "Just like back home!"

"Let's eat here," Jessie said, leading the way into the restaurant. As soon as they were all inside, Violet told her sister and brothers that they were still being followed.

"Where is he?" asked Henry, looking out the large front window of the pizzeria.

Violet looked outside, too. "I don't know where he is now, but he's been following us since we were in line for the palace."

"Do you think it's the same person from

the cab that was behind us?" asked Henry.

"I don't know. It might be," Violet answered uncertainly.

"What do you think we should do?" asked Benny.

"Should we call Grandfather?" Violet wondered.

"We don't want to bother Grandfather in the middle of his meeting, and anyway, there's no one there now," Jessie pointed out.

"I'm hungry," said Henry. "Let's order lunch."

The Aldens had a large cheese pizza. No one said anything more about the person following them, because they were all so busy eating.

When they'd finished the pizza, Violet asked, "What are we going to do this afternoon?"

Jessie wiped her fingers on a paper napkin and then took out the guidebook. She flipped through a few pages. "We could go to Madame Tussaud's Wax Museum this afternoon. It's not too far from here."

"A museum about wax?" Benny asked. "That doesn't sound very interesting."

Henry laughed. "No, it's a museum with wax figures of famous people. They look just like real people. It's supposed to be really great."

"Well, all right," Benny said doubtfully.

A little while later they arrived at Madame Tussaud's. On the way there they looked back several times, but they saw no one following them.

"Maybe I was wrong," Violet said to herself as she went into the museum.

Inside, there were several different rooms displaying wax figures of famous people. The Aldens were amazed at how lifelike they were. The figures were as large as actual people and were dressed in real clothes.

"Wow!" said Benny. "You were right — these are unbelievable!"

"They're so real," Jessie exclaimed. "I keep expecting them to move!"

There were wax figures of all sorts of people, including kings, queens, entertainers, musicians, and sports heroes.

"Look, there's Benjamin Franklin!" said Violet.

"And the Beatles!" said Henry.

"And there's Donna Russo!" cried Benny.

"What?" the others all said at the same time.

"Over there, in the corner," said Benny.

Henry, Jessie, and Violet all turned in the direction Benny was pointing. He was right. In the corner stood the unfriendly woman from their inn. She was looking closely at a wax figure of the queen.

"Benny, I thought you meant you saw a *wax* Donna," said Jessie.

"No, it's the real one," Benny said.

Suddenly Violet gasped. "Look! She's wearing a long raincoat! Could she have been the one following us?"

"I wonder. . . ." said Henry.

"Let's go say hello," suggested Jessie.

The children walked over to Donna, who was making some notes on a small notepad. As soon as she saw the children, she tucked the pad and pen into her coat pocket. The look on her face was not happy.

"Hello!" said Jessie. "Isn't it funny to run into you here!"

"Yes," said Donna. "Very funny." But she didn't seem to think it was funny at all.

"Isn't this museum great?" said Benny. "I've never seen anything like it before."

"Of course you haven't," said Donna. "This is the greatest wax museum in the world. Did you know that Madame Tussaud began making her wax figures over two hundred years ago? Of course, it wasn't *her* waxworks at the beginning; it was her uncle's. If you go into the workshop here, you can see some of the old masks and learn how the wax models are made."

"You certainly know a lot about this place," said Jessie.

Suddenly Donna seemed to realize how much she'd been talking and she became quiet.

"So . . ." Violet said slowly, "you couldn't have been here all day. What other sights did you see today?" She wanted to find out if Donna had been the one following them at Buckingham Palace.

"I don't think that's any of your business," Donna snapped, and she turned and left.

The Aldens stood watching her, stunned.

"I don't think I've ever met anyone so unfriendly!" said Violet.

"She seemed friendly when she was talking about the wax museum," Henry said. "Then all of a sudden her mood changed."

"I wonder what she was writing in that notepad before she saw us," Benny said.

"Well, we're not going to let Donna ruin our vacation," said Jessie. "Come on, let's go see that workshop she mentioned."

That night Grandfather took the children to an Indian restaurant for dinner.

The food was delicious. It was different from anything the children had ever had before, and some of it was very spicy. There were mixtures of rice and vegetables and lamb in creamy sauces.

While they ate, the children told Grandfather about all the things they'd seen that day. They also told him about the person they'd thought was following them.

"He was wearing a long raincoat," Violet said. "Then we saw Donna at the wax museum, and she was wearing one, too."

"You know, I just remembered. We've seen Andrew wearing a raincoat like that, too," Henry pointed out.

Mr. Alden pulled his raincoat from the hook next to their table. "I also have a raincoat like you described," he said. "You know, a lot of people in London have coats like that. They're good for the damp, rainy weather here. Do you think maybe it wasn't the same person you kept seeing all day, but perhaps a few different people in similar raincoats?"

The children looked at their grandfather silently.

"All I'm saying is, maybe you weren't really being followed. Maybe you just thought you were," he said gently.

"You know, Grandfather could be right," Henry said, looking around at the others.

Violet looked thoughtful. "It's possible. But there's something about this particular raincoat that looks . . . different. I just can't quite figure out what it is." Then she remembered something else. "But that cab was definitely following us."

"Maybe it was just someone else going to Buckingham Palace," said Jessie.

"I guess so," said Violet. But she wasn't convinced.

"Hey!" said Benny all of a sudden. "What about that note we got yesterday: 'A friend stopped by?' Maybe the 'friend' is the person following us."

"Could be," said Jessie. "We need to ask Mrs. Brown if she talked to her son about that."

When the Aldens returned to the inn, Mrs. Brown was in the front hallway. "Did you have fun today?" she asked.

"Yes! We saw a palace and guards marching around!" cried Benny.

"We also went to the wax museum," added Jessie. "And we saw Donna Russo there."

"She wasn't very friendly, though," said Benny.

"Don't mind her," Mrs. Brown said. "She told me she doesn't have time to chat because she's busy with a special project — her secret plan, she called it. Thinks she's going to be a millionaire, she does."

"Really?" said Henry. "What's her plan?"

"She's planning to —" Mrs. Brown stopped herself. "No. She made me promise not to tell anyone. Her idea seems like stealing to me, but she said it's not really." Mrs. Brown paused. "But enough about that. Would you all like some hot tea before bed?"

"No, thank you," Mr. Alden said.

"There is something else we were wondering about," Jessie said.

"What is it, dear?" Mrs. Brown said.

"Did you have a chance to ask your son about the 'friend' who stopped by for us yesterday?" Jessie asked.

"Oh, yes," said Mrs. Brown. "I've been meaning to tell you. My son said it was a man, and he refused to leave his name. He didn't want to leave a message at all, in fact. My son said the man was acting a bit, well, strange."

"Did your son say anything else, like what the man looked like or anything?" Henry asked.

"No, he didn't," Mrs. Brown replied.

The Aldens looked at one another and shrugged. They knew little more about the mysterious "friend" than they'd known before.

"I'm not going to worry about it," said Grandfather as they went upstairs. "If it was anyone important, he'll try us again. See you tomorrow morning." He and the children went into their rooms.

As they got ready for bed, Jessie asked Violet, "What do you think Donna Russo's 'secret plan' is all about?"

"I can't imagine!" said Violet. "Sounded pretty strange."

The girls were brushing their teeth when they heard a noise outside their door.

"Was that a knock?" Jessie asked.

"I don't know. Maybe it was Benny or Henry," Violet said. "I'll check." When she opened the door, she saw a man standing at the door across from theirs. He had a key in his hand but seemed to be having trouble unlocking the door. As he turned slightly, Violet got a glimpse of his face, and suddenly she realized it wasn't Andrew. The man in the hall had a beard.

Violet shut the door.

"Who was it?" Jessie asked her sister.

Violet didn't answer. She just stood there, looking thoughtful.

"Violet?" Jessie said.

"Oh, I'm sorry," said Violet at last. "I was just thinking. Isn't Andrew's room right across from ours?"

"Yes," said Jessie.

"There's another man at his door, trying to get into his room," Violet said.

"Trying to get in?" Jessie repeated.

"Yes. He has a key, but he's having trouble getting the door open," Violet explained.

"These old doors stick sometimes. Maybe he's a friend of Andrew's," Jessie suggested. "Or maybe Andrew checked out of the inn."

"But he said he'd be here all week," said Violet.

Jessie yawned loudly. "I don't know about you, but I'm tired." She pulled the quilt up around her.

"Me, too," said Violet, getting into her own bed. "Let's get some sleep." She turned off the light and lay back against her soft pillow. But for a long time she couldn't sleep. She kept wondering about the mysterious bearded man trying to get into Andrew's room.

CHAPTER 6

The Tower of London

The next morning, as the Aldens went down for breakfast, they saw Andrew running out the door.

"Hello!" said Jessie.

"Can't stay and chat. My limo's waiting," he called over his shoulder.

When they sat at the table, Donna was just leaving. It seemed as if she, too, had somewhere important to go.

Violet buttered a scone and then told the others about the bearded man she'd seen the night before.

"That's funny," said Benny, helping himself to another serving of scrambled eggs. "I saw an old man coming down the hall the day before yesterday."

"Sometimes people have friends or relatives visiting them," Grandfather said. "I wouldn't worry about it."

When they'd finished eating, the Aldens headed off to the oldest section of London, known as "The City." Grandfather had a business meeting there. Also, there were a couple of sights in the area that the children wanted to see.

"How about if we take the tube?" Grandfather suggested.

"Did you say the *tube*?" Benny repeated.

Grandfather chuckled.

"Isn't that what they call the subway here?" asked Henry.

"Yes. The official name is the 'underground,' " Grandfather said.

Grandfather led the way down the street to a small building like a train station. Inside, there was a ticket booth, and on the wall was a poster covered with colored lines crossing back and forth over one another.

"What's that?" Benny asked, pointing.

"That's a map showing where the tube goes," Grandfather explained. He pointed to a small circle on one of the colored lines. "This is where we are." With his finger, Grandfather followed that line to another circle on the other side of the map. "And here's where we're going, Monument Station."

Grandfather paid their fare and picked up a small folded map from the ticket booth. "Take one of these," he said, giving it to Jessie. "In case you need it later."

"Thanks," said Jessie. She tucked the map into Benny's backpack, which she was carrying over her shoulder. It still had the umbrella, guidebook, and camera inside.

The children followed Grandfather to a steep escalator that led down into the ground. When they got to the bottom there was a platform beside some train tracks. The tracks emerged from a round dark tunnel and went off into another round dark tunnel at the other end. A few moments later two lights appeared.

"Here comes the train," said Grandfather.

A train pulled up to the platform and the doors opened. After a couple of people got off, the Aldens boarded and sat down on a soft, cushioned bench. The doors closed, and the train started. It traveled for several minutes before stopping again to let people on and off.

Jessie was studying the map Grandfather had given her when a woman next to her said, "Can I help you find something?"

"No, thanks. I'm just checking to see how many stops there are before ours," Jessie replied.

"It sounds from your accent as if you're American," the woman said.

"Yes, I am," said Jessie. "We're on vacation here."

"I hope you're planning to go to the theater while you're here," the woman said. "It's the most wonderful part of London! I see every new play that opens — have for years. The very best actors perform here."

"Since you're such a fan, you may be interested to know that Andrew Smythe is staying at our inn," said Jessie.

"Andrew who?" the woman asked.

"Andrew Smythe, the actor," said Jessie.

"Never heard of him," said the woman. "Oh, here's my stop. Nice meeting you. Enjoy your visit!"

"That was odd," said Jessie, turning to the rest of her family. "That woman told me she was a big fan of the theater, but she'd never heard of Andrew."

"Really?" said Henry. "That does seem strange."

"Maybe Andrew uses a different name on stage," suggested Grandfather. "Some actors do, you know."

"Yes, I suppose that's possible," said Jessie. "But he never mentioned a stage name." She looked back at the map she was holding. "We're next, aren't we?"

"Yes," Mr. Alden said.

After leaving Monument Station, the Aldens walked a short way and then spotted a large river in front of them.

"Is that the Thames?" asked Henry.

"Yes," Grandfather said. "That's the river that runs through London. And guess what that is." He pointed straight ahead to a huge bridge.

"Is that . . . London Bridge?" Violet guessed.

"Yes, it is," said Grandfather.

"It's not falling down!" said Benny with a smile.

"I have to go this way." Grandfather pointed up the street. "But if you walk up that way, along the river, you'll get to the Tower of London. I know you'll enjoy seeing that."

"Great!" said Jessie.

The children said good-bye to Grandfather and then set off. The walk along the river was pleasant, until Violet happened to look behind them. "I hate to say it, but I think we're being followed again."

The others looked back, just in time to see a person in a long raincoat duck into a bus stop. It seemed strange that the person would be dressed like that, because it was a bright sunny day.

"Not again!" said Henry.

"Let's just hurry up and get to the tower," said Jessie.

As they got closer, Benny pointed to the high stone walls and turrets. "Wow! It's like a real castle."

Once inside the outer walls, Jessie told the others what she had read in the guidebook. "The Tower of London was begun by William the Conqueror back in 1078."

"More than nine hundred years ago!" said Henry. "That's really old!"

"Yes," said Jessie. "They built it on the river so they could watch for invaders. Other kings added to it over the years. For a long time it was used as a prison."

"A prison?" asked Benny.

"Yes. When someone committed a really bad crime, often something against the king, they'd be taken here and held in one of the towers," Jessie explained. She pointed to one of the entryways. "That's Traitor's Gate, where prisoners were brought in and had their last look at the outside world. Some people were even executed here."

"Wow," said Benny, his eyes wide.

"What's in there?" asked Henry, pointing to a large building in the center.

Jessie looked in the guidebook. "That's the White Tower. It's full of armor and weapons from hundreds of years ago."

"Let's go see!" said Benny excitedly, leading the way inside.

The children spent the next hour strolling around inside the stone building. They saw cannons, swords, muskets, and pistols of all sorts. They saw helmets and suits of armor that had belonged to kings, and even armor specially made for the horses.

"Look at this!" cried Benny, pointing to a small suit of armor. "This would fit me."

"That belonged to one of the young princes," Henry said after reading the sign on the wall.

As the children walked around, Jessie kept feeling as if someone was watching her. But whenever she turned to see, everyone just seemed to be looking at the armor.

Next the Aldens went to see the crown

jewels, the priceless jewelry and crowns that belonged to the kings and queens. As soon as Jessie entered the exhibit, she forgot all about her feeling of being watched. There were shiny, beautiful silver pieces and elegant jewelry that sparkled in the bright light. But everyone's favorites were the crowns, covered with valuable gems.

"These must be worth millions and millions of dollars," said Benny. "What if someone stole them?"

"That's why they're in these special bulletproof glass cases," Jessie said.

Henry pointed to one of the most beautiful crowns. "Queen Elizabeth II wore that crown at her coronation, the ceremony when she became queen," he read from a sign. "One day Prince Charles will wear it when he becomes king."

"That sign says the coronation crown has 3,733 precious jewels, including 2,800 diamonds!" said Violet.

"I didn't know there were that many diamonds in the whole world!" said Benny.

At the end of the exhibit, the Aldens

bought postcards in the gift shop to send to Mrs. McGregor, Aunt Jane, and some of their friends back home.

"Let's go get lunch and write our postcards," suggested Violet.

"Grandfather suggested a place near here," said Henry, leading the way. "It sells fish and chips, which is one of the most popular meals here in England."

Jessie looked back as they left the tower, to see if there was anyone following them. There were lots of people, so it was hard to see if the same raincoated stranger was among them.

At the restaurant, Henry went to the counter and ordered the fish and chips special for everyone. Meanwhile, the others settled down at a small table and began writing their postcards. When Henry came back with the tray, they all took their paper plates of food eagerly. On each plate were several pieces of batter-dipped fried fish and a pile of french fries.

"Hey, these aren't potato chips. They're french fries," said Benny.

"In England they're called chips," Henry explained.

Violet didn't usually like fish, but when she tasted hers, she found it was delicious. Benny was surprised to find that there was a bottle of vinegar to sprinkle on the french fries instead of ketchup.

As they ate, Jessie looked around and then began to talk. "I've had the feeling that someone was following us all morning. I'm getting tired of this. Why would someone follow us?"

"Maybe he's spying on us, watching what we're doing," suggested Benny.

"Or maybe we have something he wants," Violet said.

"Like what?" Jessie asked. "It just doesn't make sense."

"We've noticed a lot of things that don't make sense," said Henry. "Like the unfriendly way Donna acts."

"Andrew acted pretty strange, too, the other day," Jessie reminded them. "And it's odd that the woman on the tube hadn't heard of him."

"Do you think one of them is following us?" asked Henry. "We've seen both of them wearing raincoats."

As they talked, the children finished their lunch and got up to leave. They had just reached the door when someone familiar stepped inside. "Look, everyone!" Violet called out. "It's Charles Finchley, from the airplane!"

CHAPTER 7

"I've Hidden It. . . ."

"Hello!" Jessie said. "What are you doing here?"

"Well, if it isn't the Aldens!" said Charles. Like the first time they'd met him, he was carrying a pile of newspapers, and he had a coat draped over his arm. "How funny to run into you here! Are you enjoying your visit? What have you been doing?" he asked.

"We are," said Henry. "We've been to Buckingham Palace and saw the changing of the guard." Henry went on, "We also

visited Madame Tussaud's Wax Museum and —"

Suddenly Charles interrupted him. "Why don't you join me for lunch and you can tell me all about it."

"We've just finished eating," said Violet.

"Oh, yes, I guess you have," said Charles. He seemed at a loss for what to say next. Then suddenly his face brightened. "I've an idea," he said. "How about tea tomorrow afternoon?"

"That sounds great," said Jessie. The others nodded eagerly.

"I'll meet you at half past three at the Olde Tea Shoppe on Chiswick Lane," said Charles.

"All right, we'll see you there!" said Jessie.

When they were out on the street, Henry turned to the others. "Wasn't it a coincidence, in this whole big city, to run into Charles?"

"It sure was," said Jessie.

"It was awfully nice of him to invite us to tea, wasn't it?" Violet commented.

Quite unlike himself, Benny was walking along quietly with a worried look on his face.

"Is something wrong?" Jessie asked him at last.

"Yes," said Benny. "What am I going to do tomorrow?"

"What do you mean?" asked Jessie.

"I don't like tea!" cried Benny.

The others smiled. "They serve lots of yummy things at tea, like pastries and cookies," said Jessie. "Don't worry, you'll be just fine."

That night the Aldens ate dinner at a restaurant near their inn and then headed back to their rooms to go to bed. Jessie and Violet had just reached the door to their room when they heard a voice coming from Andrew's room.

"Yes, I've hidden it," the person was saying.

"Is that Andrew?" Jessie whispered to Violet.

Violet nodded silently.

"Don't worry!" Andrew went on angrily. "I know it's worth a lot of money. But it's in a safe place. No one will ever suspect."

"Oh, my goodness!" Jessie said, her eyes wide. She was so startled that she dropped the key to their room and it rattled on the wooden floor.

"What was that?" Andrew was saying. "I thought I heard something outside."

"Hurry!" Violet said as Jessie picked up the key and fumbled with it. She was so nervous that she dropped it on the floor again.

"Jessie!" Violet cried.

At last Jessie managed to get their door open. The two girls rushed into their room and shut the door behind them.

"Did you hear the way Andrew was talking?" Violet asked her big sister.

"Yes!" said Jessie. "He didn't sound at all like himself! He sounded so angry. And he was talking about hiding something."

Violet nodded silently.

"But he seems like such a nice man," said

Jessie. "I can't believe he would do anything wrong."

"Do you think we should do something? Tell Grandfather?" Violet asked.

"What would we tell him?" said Jessie. "That we'd been eavesdropping on Andrew and he sounded angry? We don't even know what he was talking about — or who he was talking to. I think we should just try to forget about it. It's not any of our business."

"I guess you're right," said Violet.

The next day, since they weren't meeting Charles until the afternoon, the children set out to visit Harrods, one of the largest and most famous department stores in the world.

"Why are we going shopping?" Benny wanted to know. "That doesn't sound like much fun."

"But this isn't any ordinary store," Henry explained. "This store sells *everything*."

"And afterward, Benny, we're going to buy food and take it to a park for a picnic," said Jessie.

"Now, *that* sounds like fun," said Benny.

The children spent the first part of the morning visiting several different floors in the huge store. Just as Henry had said, Harrods sold everything, from luggage to pianos.

The children were surprised to find a pet department, where they saw colorful fish in tanks and lots of pretty birds. They cuddled some tiny kittens and played with a bunch of puppies.

"These make me miss Watch," said Jessie, recalling their own dog, who was at home.

The Aldens browsed through the children's book department and spent a long time in the toy department, which contained piles of stuffed animals and games of every kind. Violet looked at the beautiful dolls in elegant dresses, while Henry, Benny, and Jessie played with the mechanical trains and remote-control cars.

There was even a children's haircutting area, and a department that sold children's furniture.

"Look at that bed shaped like a car!" said Benny, pointing.

"I like the bunk beds in the shape of a double-decker bus!" said Violet.

In the gift area the children saw a beautiful snow globe with a wooden base. Inside was a hand-carved scene of old London, with bits of glitter floating around.

"Isn't that lovely," said Violet.

"Grandfather gave us some money to buy souvenirs," said Henry. "Let's get that, and we'll all be able to enjoy it."

"Yes, we can put it on the mantel in the living room at home," suggested Violet. "Every time we see it we'll remember the wonderful time we've had here in London."

"Let's bring back something special for Mrs. McGregor, too," said Benny.

"What a thoughtful idea," said Jessie. "How about one of these?" She picked up a basket that was filled with different kinds of English tea and sweet biscuits.

"She'll love it," said Violet.

"Can we get our food for the picnic now?" asked Benny. "I'm getting hungry."

The children paid for their things and then went down to the food halls, which were bustling with crowds of people and lots of noise. There were various sections where you could buy different kinds of foods. In the bakery area Jessie and Violet picked out a loaf of crusty bread and some chocolate-covered cookies. Henry and Benny bought four red apples in the produce section and some cheese in the dairy department. In no time their picnic was complete.

After the hustle and bustle of Harrods, the Aldens were happy to walk to nearby Hyde Park, which was peaceful and quiet. They found a shady spot under a tree and sat down. Once they'd spread out their lunch, they began to eat.

"Isn't it nice that we haven't seen anyone following us today?" said Violet, who was munching a crisp apple.

"Yes," said Henry, taking a bite of bread and cheese.

Jessie had been digging around in Benny's backpack, which they'd brought with them, as usual. At last she pulled out a colorful brochure. "Tonight's the night we're going to the theater. Grandfather gave me this listing of all the current shows so that we can read about the one we're going to."

"Is it Andrew's show? *The Mystery Man*?" asked Benny.

"No, Grandfather said that one was sold out," said Jessie. "But speaking of Andrew, Violet and I heard something very strange last night." She and Violet told their brothers what they'd overheard.

"That doesn't sound like Andrew," said Henry. "Maybe there's a side of him we don't know."

"It was very strange," said Jessie. "He sounded almost like a different person."

"Maybe it was a different person!" cried Benny. "Maybe it was the man with the beard! Or the old man!"

Violet and Jessie thought for a moment. "I guess it could have been someone else," said Jessie after a while. "I just assumed it was Andrew, since it was his room. Maybe he had a friend with him."

"I don't know," said Violet. "But it was scary."

Jessie didn't want her sister to be frightened, so she quickly changed the subject. "Anyway, tonight we're going to see *A Tale of Magic.*" Jessie read from the brochure, "It says, '*An exciting story about a group of children who take a magical journey to solve a mystery.*'"

"That sounds great!" Benny said. "What does it say there about Andrew's show?"

Jessie looked down the list of plays. "That's strange," she said. "I see it listed here, but I don't see Andrew's name. Didn't he say he was the star?"

"Yes," said Violet.

"It says here that the star is someone named Ambrose Prince," Jessie said.

"That could be Andrew's stage name," suggested Henry. "Or maybe the listing you're reading is out of date. Maybe Ambrose Prince quit the show and Andrew is the new star."

"Maybe," said Jessie. "Or maybe Andrew wasn't telling us the truth. After what we heard last night, I don't know what to think.

And remember that woman on the tube yesterday, who knew so much about the theater but hadn't heard of Andrew?"

Violet sighed. "I wonder if Andrew's up to something that he doesn't want anyone to know about."

"You may be right," said Henry.

"It seems like everyone at our inn is up to something," said Jessie. "Remember Mrs. Brown said Donna has a 'secret plan'?"

"What do you think it could be?" asked Benny.

"Who knows," said Henry. "But I guess that explains why she's always acting so secretive."

When they'd finished eating, the Aldens strolled about the pathways that crisscrossed the park. Their walk led them into another park called Kensington Gardens, where they saw several statues. Henry liked one of a man riding on a horse, while Violet's favorite was of Peter Pan. "It says on this plaque that the man who wrote the book *Peter Pan* lived near here," she said excitedly. "I love that book!"

A little farther on, they came across a large pond, where they watched people sailing model boats and fed their leftover crusts of bread to a family of ducks. There was also a playground, where they stayed until it was time to go meet Charles for tea.

CHAPTER 8

Afternoon Tea

The night before, Grandfather had helped the children locate Chiswick Lane on a map. It was a small street close to Kensington Gardens. It took only about ten minutes to walk there from the playground.

"There's the tea shop," said Violet, pointing to a storefront with a big glass window and lovely lace curtains. When the children entered they found a room with several small tables and a long buffet at the back.

Charles was already there, sitting at a table near the window.

"Hello!" the children called out as they went to sit down with him.

"Good to see you!" Charles said with a big smile. There was a small pot of tea on the table, and as he poured himself a cup, his hand shook and tea spilled onto the table. "Oh, dear, look what a mess I'm making," Charles said, reaching for his napkin to wipe up the spill. But in cleaning it up, his hand knocked the teacup and more tea spilled out.

"Let me help you," Violet said. She wondered why Charles seemed so nervous.

Just then a waitress came to the table. "I'll take care of that, Mr. Finchley," she said, clearing away the spilled teacup and wiping the table. "There. Would you children like some tea as well, or would you prefer hot cocoa?"

"Hot cocoa!" cried Benny. The others nodded eagerly.

"Four cups of cocoa, Doris," Charles told the waitress.

"Help yourself to the buffet whenever you're ready," she told them and walked away.

"This is my favorite tea shop," said Charles. "I come here quite often to enjoy the wonderful buffet. Why don't you all go up and pick out whatever you'd like." He motioned to the long table in the back.

"Okay," said Benny, springing up from the table. He could see an assortment of cakes from where they were sitting. The others got up, also.

"Aren't you coming?" Jessie asked when she noticed that Charles was still seated.

"No, I'll just have tea right now," he said.

"If you're not going up, I'll stay here, too, and —" Jessie began.

"No, no, no — please — go ahead," Charles said quickly. He seemed upset, but then he collected himself. "Really, I'm quite comfortable by myself."

"All right," said Jessie, following the others. She wondered what was bothering Charles.

The buffet was indeed wonderful, as

Charles had said. At one end there were tiny sandwiches filled with cucumber, cheese, or egg salad. They were made on very thin bread and cut into pretty shapes like hearts and diamonds.

Beside the tea sandwiches was a basket of scones, surrounded by several dishes of jam. Next came the pastries and cakes, which were layered with chocolate, whipped cream, and fruit fillings.

"I want one of everything!" said Benny.

"You may have that if you like," said Doris as she walked by, carrying a tray of hot cocoa to their table.

"Why don't you start with just a few things," said Jessie. "You can always come back for more."

"Look at that cake," said Benny, pointing to a cake at the end of the buffet. It was elaborately decorated with swirls of chocolate icing and large red strawberries. He'd never seen a cake so fancy — or so delicious-looking. "Do you think Mrs. McGregor could make one like that for my next birthday?"

"I'm sure she could. She's such a good cook. Just tell her about it when we get home," said Violet.

"I have a good idea," said Benny. "I'll take a picture of it!" He headed back to the table to get the camera out of his backpack. When he got there, Charles looked surprised to see him.

"Oh, hello — aren't you having anything for tea?" Charles asked.

"I want to take a picture of one of those cakes first," Benny said. He reached under the chair he'd been sitting in. "That's funny." He looked under the chair. "I thought I left my backpack right here."

"Oh, here it is," said Charles, pulling the backpack up from under the table. "Somehow it got pushed over to my side of the table."

"Thanks," said Benny. He took out his camera and went back to the buffet.

A moment later, the Aldens returned to the table, their plates piled with goodies.

"We brought some extra sandwiches and scones for you," said Jessie.

"How thoughtful," said Charles.

As the Aldens tasted each of the items from the buffet, they chatted with Charles about their sightseeing. They told him what a wonderful time they'd had at Buckingham Palace and Harrods, and how excited they were about the play they were seeing that night. While he seemed friendly enough, the Aldens couldn't help noticing that Charles didn't seem to be paying complete attention to them. It seemed as if he was thinking about something else.

They were almost done eating when Henry said, "One strange thing has happened during our visit."

"Really?" said Charles. "What's that?"

"Several times we thought we saw someone following us," Henry explained.

"That is odd," said Charles. All of a sudden he looked at his watch. "Oh, dear, I've just remembered I have an appointment." He motioned to Doris, who brought the check. "Take your time and stay as long as you like," he told the Aldens as he put on his wrinkled raincoat. "Bye-bye!"

"Good-bye," the Aldens called after him.

"He certainly left in a hurry," said Jessie.

"Yes, and just when I was telling him about the person following us around," said Henry. "All of a sudden he looked very uncomfortable."

"Probably because he just realized he'd forgotten his appointment," said Violet.

"I guess so," said Henry. But he didn't seem satisfied.

"I know something else he forgot," said Benny. He reached under the table and pulled something out. "His hat!"

After tea the Aldens returned to their inn, bringing Charles's hat with them. They hoped they might be able to return it to him before leaving London. Back at the inn they changed into nice clothes for the theater. Benny and Henry put on khaki slacks, loafers, and clean white shirts. The girls wore flowered dresses and put bows in their hair. Jessie's bow was red and Violet's was purple, her favorite color. Grandfather had on a gray suit, with his pocket watch tucked into his vest. They looked so nice that when they passed Donna as they were leaving, she even smiled and told them to enjoy the show.

The evening was just as wonderful as they had hoped it would be. The theater was old and quite elegant, with an ornately carved ceiling and a thick red velvet curtain. The show was exciting, and all the actors and actresses were very good. The children all liked the beautiful scenery and costumes, but their favorite parts were the songs and dances.

"Thank you for taking us to the play, Grandfather," said Henry as they got into their cab at the end of the night.

"It was great," Violet added.

The Aldens were all quite tired when they reached the inn. They'd had a busy day.

"I can't wait to go to sleep," said Benny.

"That's a switch," said Grandfather, chuckling. Usually Benny wanted to stay up as late as possible.

But when Henry opened the door to

their room, the boys were in for a shock. The pillows and blankets had been pulled off their beds and the contents of their drawers had been dumped out on the floor.

"Grandfather!" Henry called. "We've been robbed!"

CHAPTER 9

A Hidden Package

The Aldens gathered in the door of Benny and Henry's room, looking at the mess inside. The girls had heard the commotion and had come back to see what was going on. "Who would have done such a thing?" asked Violet.

"Run downstairs and see if you can find Mrs. Brown," Grandfather told Henry. "In the meantime, we'll check the other rooms and make sure they're okay."

It turned out that only the boys' room had been broken into. "We'd better not

touch anything until the police come," said Grandfather.

Mrs. Brown had been down in the kitchen preparing for breakfast the next day. When she saw what had happened to the boys' room, she gasped and put her hands to her mouth. "Oh, my word!" she said. "Nothing like this has ever happened here before!" She hurried to call the police. In a few minutes, an officer had arrived.

"Is he a policeman?" Benny whispered to Henry. He didn't look like the police back home. He had on a black uniform and a tall curved hat.

"Yes," said Henry. "He's a bobby."

"How do you know his name is Bobby?" Benny asked.

"That's not his name; that's what police officers are called here," Henry explained.

The bobby asked the Aldens some questions and made notes in a small notebook. "Does anything appear to be missing?"

The boys looked through the piles of things that had been dumped from the drawers.

"I don't think so," said Henry. "We didn't have anything valuable here, anyway. I had my money with me at the play."

"Wait a minute!" said Benny. "There *is* something missing! My backpack!"

"Here's your backpack," said Jessie, handing it him. "You left it in our room. The camera is still inside."

Benny took the backpack, a look of relief on his face.

"How did the burglar get in?" Grandfather wanted to know.

"These locks are pretty easy to pick," said the bobby. "It could have been someone who works here, or one of the other guests. Or maybe someone sneaked in the front door when Mrs. Brown wasn't around."

"My family and I are the only ones who work here," Mrs. Brown said. "And I can't believe it was one of my guests. I suppose someone could have sneaked in — I've never had a problem like this, so I usually don't lock the front door until I go to bed. Still, I can't believe someone could have come in without my knowing."

"It's late now, so I'll come back tomorrow morning to speak to the other guests," the bobby said. "I'll find out if anyone heard or saw anything suspicious."

Mr. Alden went with Mrs. Brown to show the bobby out, while the girls helped Benny and Henry put everything back where it belonged. At last their room was in order.

"We'll have to make sure we don't leave any valuables lying around until they catch the person who did this," said Jessie.

"I'll put my money in Benny's backpack for safekeeping," said Henry. "I'll just tuck it in this outside pocket."

As Henry unzipped the pocket and reached inside, the look on his face changed. "Hey, what's this?" He pulled out a small wrapped bundle.

The Aldens crowded around to see what Henry was holding. The package was flat and about three inches square. It was tightly wrapped and taped. "Did anyone put this in here?" asked Henry.

They all shook their heads.

"What is it?" asked Benny.

Slowly Henry pulled off the tape and began to unwrap the package. Pulling off the paper, he uncovered a small sturdy box. The children were becoming more and more curious. When Henry opened the box, they all opened their eyes wide in surprise. Inside was a shiny gold brooch covered with diamonds and other sparkling gems. The letters *HRH* were engraved in the center. It was obviously quite old.

"That looks really valuable," said Benny. "I wonder whose initials those are."

"Those aren't just someone's initials!" said Henry. "That stands for 'Her Royal Highness.' This must have belonged to . . . a queen!"

"Oh, my goodness!" said Jessie.

"It looks familiar," said Violet.

"Familiar?" Jessie repeated.

"Yes, I think I've seen something just like it, but I'm not sure where," Violet explained.

"What I want to know is, how did it get into my backpack?" Benny asked.

"It was inside that zipped pocket, so it

couldn't have just fallen in," said Henry. "Someone must have put it there on purpose."

"And he came back for it tonight!" Violet exclaimed. "Maybe that's what the thief was after! He assumed the backpack was in Benny's room, so he broke in. He didn't know it was in *our* room."

"I was wondering why ours was the only room that was burglarized," said Henry. "That would explain it — he wasn't just looking for anything valuable, he was looking for one thing in particular, and thought it would only be in here."

Suddenly Jessie gasped. "Maybe that's why someone's been following us! Like Violet said the other day, he was following us because we had something he wanted. He's been trying to get it back all week! We've had the backpack with us every day. This is one of the first times we've left it and gone out at night."

"Why did he break into our room tonight and not before?" asked Benny.

"Somehow it seems as if the person knew

we'd be out tonight and probably wouldn't be bringing the backpack," said Henry.

"But who would have known that?" asked Benny.

"We told Andrew we'd be going to the theater tonight," said Jessie. "And remember what he said about hiding something where it would be safe!"

"He does seem like the most likely suspect," said Henry. "But don't forget Donna. She saw us as we were leaving the inn tonight. And Mrs. Brown said something about her having a secret plan to get rich. If she stole this brooch and sold it, she'd be rich."

"Mrs. Brown even said her plan was sort of like stealing," Benny added.

"I just thought of someone else," Jessie said. "We told Charles we were going to the theater tonight, too."

"But he's such a kind man," said Violet. "I can't believe he'd do anything like this."

When Mr. Alden came back downstairs, the children showed him the brooch. He turned it over in his hands, studying it. He was just as mystified as they were.

At last he said, "I have a very important meeting first thing tomorrow morning, and I've got to get some sleep. But as soon as my meeting's over, we'll all go to the police station and show them this brooch. Maybe someone has reported it missing. At any rate, the police will know what to do. For now I think the best thing is to get some sleep." He turned to the boys. "I think it's safe to sleep here. Whoever broke in didn't find what he was looking for. I'm sure he won't come back."

"And you'll be right across the hall if we need you," said Benny, yawning loudly.

"Yes," said Grandfather. "Good night."

But although it was very late and they were all tired, a long time passed before any of the Aldens could fall asleep.

CHAPTER 10

Mystery Solved!

After all the late-night excite-
ment, the children slept late the next morning. When they awoke, their grandfather had
already left for his business meeting. He'd
left a note telling them when he'd be home
and how to reach him if they needed to.

Because it was so late, the Aldens were
the only ones at breakfast. Mrs. Brown told
them that the bobby had spoken to Andrew
and Donna earlier, but there was no new information.

Jessie turned to the others. "Grandfather

probably won't be back until this afternoon, so what should we do until then?"

"How about going to a museum?" suggested Henry. "There are lots in London and so far we've only been to one, the British Museum."

"That's it!" said Violet.

Everyone turned to look at her.

"That's why that brooch looks familiar," Violet said. "Remember that jewelry exhibit at the British Museum we saw on our first day here? There were some earrings there that looked just like the brooch — they're probably a matching set!"

"Let's go back there and take a look," said Jessie. "Maybe there's someone who works at the museum we could talk to."

The Aldens finished eating quickly and left the inn. They brought the brooch with them, wrapped up and tucked carefully in Jessie's pocket.

At the museum they went straight to the glass display case that held the antique jewelry.

"Look!" said Jessie, pointing. "Violet was

right. Those earrings are a perfect match for the brooch."

The children all peered into the case in amazement. The earrings were the same oval shape, with the same jewels and intricately engraved *HRH*.

"It says they belonged to Queen Victoria over one hundred years ago," said Violet. "Do you think the brooch did, too?"

"We'd better speak to someone in charge," said Henry, heading to the information desk. "Hello, we'd like to speak to someone about the royal jewelry," he said to the woman who was sitting there. "It's important."

The woman studied Henry for a moment. She was obviously trying to decide whether he was serious.

"We've found something that may be worth a lot of money," Jessie added.

The woman at the desk picked up her telephone and dialed. "Mrs. Scherr, there are some children here who want to see you, if you have a moment. I know you're busy, but they say it's important." She

listened for a moment and hung up the phone. Then she motioned to one of the uniformed security guards. "Please take these children to speak to Mrs. Scherr," she said. "She's the head of the British Antiques Department," she told the Aldens.

The guard led them to the section of the museum where the offices were. "Here's Mrs. Scherr's office," he said.

"Thanks," said Jessie as the children went inside.

A dark-haired woman was sitting behind a large desk, which was covered with books and papers. She smiled when she saw the Aldens. "Can I help you?"

"We found something that may belong in this museum," Jessie said, pulling the package out of her pocket and laying it on the desk.

Mrs. Scherr looked at the children curiously and then began unwrapping the package. When she saw the brooch she gasped. "But — but — wherever did you find this?"

"I know this is going to sound strange," Henry began. "It was tucked inside my little brother's backpack."

Benny smiled proudly and held up the red backpack.

"How did it get there?" Mrs. Scherr asked.

"We have no idea," said Jessie.

"This is a very valuable brooch," Mrs. Scherr explained. "It belonged to Queen Victoria. It's part of a set."

"It goes with the earrings in the glass display case, doesn't it?" asked Violet.

"Yes," said Mrs. Scherr. "This brooch was in a private collection. Last week it was auctioned — in America. I sent my assistant to purchase it for the museum, and he's due back next week. I can't imagine how the brooch ended up in your backpack!"

"We were just as surprised as you are," said Jessie.

Suddenly Benny said, "What is your assistant's name?"

"My assistant?" Mrs. Scherr asked. She sounded surprised at the question. "His name is Charles. Charles Finchley."

"Charles?" said Jessie and Henry at the same time.

"I think I know what happened," said Benny.

Everyone turned to Benny.

"Remember Charles was sitting right near us on the plane, and he had a red backpack just like mine?" Benny said.

"That's right!" said Jessie. "He did."

Benny went on, "The backpacks were both in the overhead bin during the flight and —"

"And I put the brooch in the wrong backpack," said a voice in the doorway.

Everyone turned to see Charles standing there, his head down.

"Charles, what is going on?" Mrs. Scherr demanded.

"I'm so sorry, Lauren. I never meant for this to happen," said Charles. "I went to the auction and bought the brooch, just as I told you on the telephone. But I was so excited I wanted to bring it back myself to surprise you. So I caught an earlier flight. Midway through the flight I took the brooch out to make sure it was safe, and then I returned it to my backpack. It wasn't until I got home that I realized I'd put it in the wrong bag. I'm so scatter-brained sometimes."

"You certainly are," Mrs. Scherr agreed, but her voice was gentle.

"So why didn't you tell us?" asked Jessie. "We would have given it back to you."

"I started to," said Charles. "I came by your hotel, but you weren't in. And then I panicked. I was afraid that if anyone found out what I'd done, I'd lose my job here."

"So you were the friend who stopped by," said Jessie, beginning to understand.

"Then you followed us around, trying to get it back," said Henry. "We saw someone in a raincoat —"

"That's what was different about the rain-coat," said Violet. "It was all wrinkled!"

"Yes," Charles said. "That was me. I hoped you'd put your backpack down and I could quickly take out the brooch without bothering anyone. No one would ever know. I tried to get it during tea."

"So that's why my bag wasn't under my

chair when I went to get the camera," said Benny.

"We mentioned we were going to the theater last night," said Jessie, "and so you took the opportunity to break into Benny's room."

"I've never done anything like that before, but I was getting desperate," Charles said, his voice cracking. "That brooch is very valuable — I had to get it back! Last night, when I didn't find it, I finally realized I had to tell the truth. I should have done that in the first place. That's why I came here, Lauren. I was going to tell you everything." Charles sighed heavily. "I guess you'll want to call the police now."

Mrs. Scherr looked seriously at Charles. "I don't know. I don't know what to do."

Everyone sat silently as Mrs. Scherr picked up the brooch and studied it.

Then Violet spoke up in a quiet voice. "Charles, what you did was wrong — following us around, breaking into Benny and Henry's room. You really scared us! Still, you must have been very frightened, having lost something so valuable. You must not have thought about what you were doing." Violet looked at her sister and brothers, and then back at Charles. "I think we can forgive you." The others nodded.

"And for me," Mrs. Scherr said, "the important thing is that the brooch is safe and you've told me the truth. You do excellent work, Charles — most of the time. I'd hate to lose you." Mrs. Scherr paused. "I think we can put this all behind us."

"You mean you're not going to report me to the police?" Charles said. "Or fire me?"

"No," said Mrs. Scherr. "But I'm certainly not sending you to any more auctions. From now on you can just work here in the office."

"Oh, thank you, Lauren," Charles said. "I won't make you sorry."

"I just remembered," Violet said. "We have something that belongs to you, Charles."

"You do?" Charles asked.

"Yes, your hat," said Violet. "You left it in the tea shop."

"That's right," said Benny, digging into his backpack and pulling it out. He handed it to Charles.

"So that's what I did with it! What would I do without kind people like you?" Charles asked, turning his hat around in his hands. "If that brooch had ended up in someone else's bag, they might have kept it, or sold it for lots of money. Even if they were honest people, they might not have known where to return it. I'm lucky you children are so honest and that you were clever enough to figure out that the brooch belonged here at the museum." Placing his hat on a table beside him, he walked over to the Aldens. One by one he shook each of their hands. "Thank you again," he said warmly. "When do you leave London?"

"On Monday, at three o'clock," said Jessie.

"Have a safe trip," Charles said. Then he turned back to Lauren. "Now, do you mind if I go call my wife and tell her that everything's going to be all right?"

"Not at all," Mrs. Scherr said.

With that, Charles hurried out of the office. No sooner had he left than Benny picked up a hat from the table that Charles had been standing next to. "Wait," he called out the door. "You forgot something!"

Everybody laughed.

That afternoon, when Mr. Alden got back from his meeting, Mrs. Brown served the family tea and cookies in the living room. The children told their grandfather all about what had happened at the museum. They had left the brooch with Mrs. Scherr and were happy to have solved the mystery at last.

"There's just one thing I'm wondering," said Jessie. "If Andrew wasn't the one who hid the brooch in the backpack, then what did he mean about hiding something where no one would ever find it?"

"I guess we may never know," said Henry.

Just then they heard the front door shut. "Hello, hello! Anyone here?" Andrew called, bounding into the living room. "I have wonderful news! I'm going to be famous! A star of the stage!"

"But you said you were already a star!" said Jessie, confused.

"I did tell you that, didn't I?" said Andrew apologetically. "That was a bit of an exaggeration. But I will be a star soon!"

"What do you mean?" asked Henry. "You said you'd been in all those shows! Are you a famous actor or not?"

"Actor, yes. Famous, no," said Andrew. "At least, *not yet*. You thought I was famous because I was wearing dark glasses. I couldn't resist — I'm an actor, I love to become someone I'm not. So I pretended to be a star."

"So that's why that theater fan hadn't heard of you," said Jessie.

"And that's why you looked uncomfortable when we said we might go to your show," said Benny. "We would have found out you were lying."

"But it wasn't all a lie," said Andrew. "I *have* been in lots of shows, but only in small-town theaters. I came to London a few weeks ago, hoping to finally make it big. I've been auditioning for lots of different parts, dressing up, practicing the lines in my room —"

"Wait a minute, did you say dressing up?" asked Benny. "Like an old man? Or someone with a beard?"

"Yes," Andrew said. "Sometimes it helps me if I dress the part I'm auditioning for."

"And you've been practicing your lines in your room?" Jessie asked. "Saying you were hiding something where no one would ever suspect?"

"Yes," said Andrew, smiling broadly. "That's from *The Mystery Man.*"

"We heard you, and you didn't sound at all like yourself!" said Violet.

"That's good, because I was pretending to be a gangster — Ambrose Prince's part. I've just found out he's leaving the show, and I'm taking over the starring role. It's a dream come true!"

"Speaking of dreams, I have some news of my own," said Donna, who had just entered the living room.

Everyone turned to look at her. She was

carrying a small stack of fliers, which she passed around.

" '*Opening Soon: Madame Russo's Wax Museum*,' " said Jessie, reading aloud.

"I'm opening my own museum back in the United States," said Donna. "I just found a location for it, and I've signed all the papers to get it started. One day my museum will be as famous as Madame Tussaud's."

"So this is your secret plan to get rich," said Benny.

"And that's why you knew so much about the wax museum," Violet added.

"Yes," Donna said. "I've been reading books about waxworks and visiting there every day. But I didn't want anyone to know, because I was afraid someone might steal my idea before I'd gotten everything arranged."

"Aren't there already wax museums in the United States?" asked Benny.

"There are, but none is as popular as Madame Tussaud's. *Mine* will be," Donna said.

The guests at the Cheshire Inn spent the rest of the afternoon celebrating their successes. Andrew had gotten a starring role in a play. Donna's wax museum would be opening soon. And the Aldens had solved yet another mystery.

On Monday morning, the Aldens packed up their suitcases and said good-bye to Donna, Andrew, and Mrs. Brown. They were quite sad to be leaving London. They had had such a good time.

Mrs. Brown had called for a cab to drive them to the airport. When they arrived there, a porter took their luggage, except for the pieces they were carrying on with them, like Benny's red backpack.

Jessie found a television screen that listed all the departing flights. "There's ours," she said. "It's leaving from gate 6A."

"That's this way," said Henry, pointing down a long hallway. The Aldens walked until they came to a counter with a sign over it saying "6A." Behind the counter stood a woman in an airline uniform. Grandfather handed her their tickets and she checked them in.

"Is that our plane?" Benny asked, looking out a large window.

"Yes," the woman said. "We'll be boarding in a few minutes."

The Aldens took their carry-on bags over to a group of chairs by the window. They had just sat down when a voice right behind them said, "Hello, Aldens!" Grandfather and the children turned around to see Charles Finchley.

"Charles! What are you doing here?" asked Jessie.

"I came to see you off!" said Charles with a big smile. "I can only stay a few minutes, because I have to get back to the museum." He took off his wrinkled raincoat and hat and laid them on a chair. Then he pulled a crumpled piece of paper from his pocket. "I'd like to exchange addresses, so that we can stay in touch."

"That would be nice," said Violet.

Charles picked up his raincoat and checked all the pockets. "Oh, dear, I seem to have forgotten my pen."

"I've got one," Benny said, reaching into his red backpack and pulling out a blue marker.

Charles tore the paper in half and wrote his name and address on one piece. Then he gave the other piece of paper and the marker to Henry, who wrote down the Aldens' address. Then they traded papers.

"We'll write as soon as we get home!" said Jessie.

"And I can paint you a picture," said Violet.

"We could even write you a letter on the airplane!" Benny said.

"That sounds lovely." Charles sat for a few minutes with the Aldens, watching the airplanes landing and taking off. Then he looked at his watch. "I'd better be going now," he said, pulling on his raincoat. Then Aldens waved good-bye as Charles headed down the hallway.

"Flight 125 is now boarding," a voice said over the loudspeaker.

"That's us," said Jessie.

As the Aldens turned back to their seats to collect their things, they spotted something on one of the chairs. It was Charles's hat.

"Oh, no!" said Benny. "Not again!"

JUN -- 2014

GERTRUDE CHANDLER WARNER discovered when she was teaching that many readers who like an exciting story could find no books that were both easy and fun to read. She decided to try to meet this need, and her first book, *The Boxcar Children*, quickly proved she had succeeded.

Miss Warner drew on her own experiences to write the mystery. As a child she spent hours watching trains go by on the tracks opposite her family home. She often dreamed about what it would be like to set up housekeeping in a caboose or freight car — the situation the Alden children find themselves in.

When Miss Warner received requests for more adventures involving Henry, Jessie, Violet, and Benny Alden, she began additional stories. In each, she chose a special setting and introduced unusual or eccentric characters who liked the unpredictable.

While the mystery element is central to each of Miss Warner's books, she never thought of them as strictly juvenile mysteries. She liked to stress the Aldens' independence and resourcefulness and their solid New England devotion to using up and making do. The Aldens go about most of their adventures with as little adult supervision as possible — something else that delights young readers.

Miss Warner lived in Putnam, Connecticut, until her death in 1979. During her lifetime, she received hundreds of letters from girls and boys telling her how much they liked her books.